BAMBERT'S
BOOK OF
MISSING STORIES

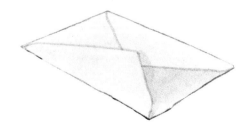

Also by Reinhardt Jung

DREAMING IN BLACK AND WHITE

For Fia and Piers
E.C.C.

EGMONT
We bring stories to life

First published 2008
by Egmont UK Limited
239 Kensington High Street, London W8 6SA

Text copyright © Reinhardt Jung
Illustrations copyright © Emma Chichester Clark 2008
All rights reserved.
Reinhardt Jung and Emma Chichester Clark have asserted their moral rights.

ISBN HB 9 7814 0523 640 9

A CIP catalogue record for this title
is available from The British Library

1 3 5 7 9 10 8 6 4 2

Printed in Singapore

BAMBERT'S BOOK OF MISSING STORIES

REINHARDT JUNG

ILLUSTRATED BY

EMMA CHICHESTER CLARK

TRANSLATED BY ANTHEA BELL

CONTENTS

BAMBERT was a very short man. His head sat on his shoulders with almost no neck in between, he couldn't walk without a stick, and even then it was painful for him to get about.

His walking-stick had a gold knob. The rest of it was black, and it helped him to make his way through life.

Although he was so small of stature, Bambert was a great writer, but no one knew it except himself – he had never let anyone else read one of his stories. None the less, he was not really lonely: he had his stories to keep him company. They came to life in him alone, and only in those stories could Bambert travel through space and time as no one had ever done before.

He couldn't really travel because of the pain in his hips, and he no longer expected any help from the doctors at whose hands he had suffered in many ways throughout his childhood. They had stretched his sinews and his skin, broken bones, straightened and re-set them – until at last they had to admit that Bambert would never be any taller, and must resign himself to that fate when he grew up. Bambert felt like a shipwrecked mariner cast up on hostile shores on the far side of a dream. This world was purgatory to him. Over there on the other side was his lost paradise.

After his parents' death, Bambert had put all his money together and adapted the family house to suit himself. He let Mr Bloom the grocer go on keeping his shop on the ground floor, but he converted everything above it, all the way up to the roof. He had furniture specially made the right size for him, and rails fitted to the stairs with an electric chairlift to carry him easily and painlessly up to the attic window, where he sometimes liked to sit enjoying the sense of the wide-open space outside.

Bambert particularly liked sitting up there at night, holding quiet conversations with the moon, for the moon, which seemed to know as many stories as Bambert himself, acted as a mirror in which he could see the world.

Out of that bright looking-glass, stories flew down to Bambert, and by day he wrote them down in a big book, which he called his *Book of Wishes*.

Bambert was very well educated. What he described as his 'little library' contained over a thousand books, and he had read every one of them. He saw the world through the eyes of poets and writers, but the world, for its own part, knew nothing about Bambert's own quiet life.

Like everyone else, Bambert read the newspaper, but since he felt panic-stricken when pictures passed rapidly before his eyes he avoided television. The violence of major news events made him feel helpless, and the oddity of the idea that they were all going on at the same time made him feel small. So Bambert would not have television in the house. It seemed to him a delusion designed as a personal attack on him and his small footsteps, and his preference for all that went slowly.

Mr Bloom the shopkeeper sent food and drink up from the ground floor in a lift which Bambert had fitted.

Bambert hardly ever left the house. He always feared that adults would pity him and children would laugh at him, for like the people at the employment centre they recognised Bambert as someone who was grown up, but still wore children's clothes.

As a writer, Bambert remained unknown. The employment centre offered him nothing but jobs exploiting his short stature. But he felt he could do without that kind of job: he didn't want to be one of the Seven Dwarves in a fairy-tale theme park, or show off his small height to amuse the audience at a variety show. Not that Bambert had anything against dwarves, but he was a human being and a writer too, and while he might be deformed he also had backbone.

One day Bambert happened to be sitting looking at his *Book of Wishes* when he saw that there was space left for only one story. That last story, thought Bambert, should be very special! It must be a true story, it must really happen, it mustn't just be invented and written down. But how could he make his stories come true?

That night the sky was overcast, and the moon refused to answer Bambert's question. All of a sudden he felt as if the stories which used to wander through his head at their leisure were caught and frozen in the *Book of Wishes*.

Making a story come true would mean letting it out of the book to go off into the world and look for its own setting, searching for cities, riverbanks, sea shores: places where it could come to life in real human beings, against real landscapes and within real walls.

That was the night when Bambert decided to tear up his *Book of Wishes* into its separate parts.

Freed from their cover, the separate stories now lay in front of Bambert, and he sent an order for ink eradicator down to Mr Bloom the shopkeeper.

The order came back up to Bambert's kitchen in the lift, and he started work at once, releasing his stories from the constraint of being set in any particular place. Bambert felt sure that the stories were strong enough to find their own settings for themselves. However, he left the people in his stories alone. Eradicating the characters would have felt like murder.

The very last story in the torn-up book consisted of four sheets of blank paper on which Bambert had not yet written anything. But because he secretly hoped that this last story might actually write itself if only it tried, he stapled the four blank sheets together too. He had now stapled each of the eleven stories together, folded them and put them in separate envelopes.

Bambert immediately sent another order down in the lift. Old Mr Bloom was surprised when he read the note telling him what Bambert wanted. It asked:

Please get me eleven Japanese tissue paper hot-air balloons, powered by tea-lights, which can fly a very long way.

Bambert.

Bambert had to wait almost two weeks before Mr Bloom the shopkeeper finally sent the folded hot-air balloons from Japan and their tea-lights up in the lift.

Meanwhile Bambert drafted the letter which he planned to send with his stories when they went on their travels. It said that he, Bambert, was letting his stories go out into the world to find their own settings, settings to suit the characters. Would the finders please send him back the stories and tell him where they had been discovered? For not until he, Bambert, knew where his stories had put down roots could he collect them all in a book again.

He promised to send a copy of the book to the finder of each story, signed his name and added his address: care of Mr Bloom, Retail and Wholesale Groceries.

Bambert put a copy of this letter in with each of his stories, even the last, which was just blank pages. It was his bold idea that an unwritten story needed to find the right setting even more than the others.

Now he was waiting for the nights to turn cold, since common sense told him that cold weather would carry his hot-air balloons higher and take them further than any mild and gentle breeze.

And at last the weather was right: a keen east wind was dusting frost over the city rooftops when Bambert got on the stairlift and took his hot-air balloons up to the attic window. It was about three in the morning, because Bambert did not want to attract any attention, and he also thought that at this dead hour the crows and aeroplanes, which might endanger his tissue paper hot-air balloons, would not be around. The balloons were thin-skinned, and their flight was gentle and graceful.

He sent the first three stories flying away that night. They floated out of the open attic window, rose slowly into the night sky, and finally disappeared behind the clouds like faint little moons. Bambert was happier than he had ever been in his whole life.

By the time Bambert saw his last story, the one with the blank pages, float out of the attic window it was February, and the night wind had changed direction quite often. The moment was still a solemn one. But now his long wait began. Bambert had already opened his atlas many times to trace the direction of the winds with his finger, wondering where they might have carried which of his stories.

Spring and summer passed, autumn gales were rattling the tiles on the rooftops, and still Bambert had no news of the setting of even one of his stories.

He began to feel anxious: how many of the stories might the sea have swallowed up? How many might be hanging out of reach at the top of a tree? He told himself it had been stupid to entrust his stories to the wind.

Now he grew impatient.

Night after night he paced up and down, leaning on his stick and feeling angry with himself. He had no appetite, and lost weight.

Mr Bloom the shopkeeper always sent him up three rolls for breakfast, but these days Bambert would put two back in the lift and send them down again. Instead, he drank more coffee than ever before.

Slowly, the *Book of Wishes* turned into a *Book of Missing Stories*.

It was winter again when Mr Bloom the shopkeeper sent the lift up to Bambert at about twelve noon one day. He was sitting at the table with his atlas in front of him, and he did not even look up when the lift opened. He didn't feel hungry; he didn't want any lunch. He was going to send the lift straight back down to Mr Bloom when he saw the envelope inside it. An envelope with foreign stamps and clumsy handwriting.

Suddenly he felt hot, and his hands trembled. Hardly daring to believe it, he took the envelope out of the lift and put it on the table in front of him.

The letter came from Donegal Bay in Ireland, and the stamps were postmarked Dublin. Which of his stories had found its setting in Ireland?

Bambert tore the envelope open and found the tale of *The Eye in the Sea*.

He unfolded his old manuscript, and entered the words 'Ireland' and 'Donegal Bay'. He used Irish names for the characters, and when he read his story again it seemed as if it must always have been set in Ireland:

THE EYE IN THE SEA

Once upon a time there was a boy who lived on the west coast of Ireland. His father was out of work, and every morning the boy went down to the beach at low tide to collect the flotsam and jetsam cast ashore overnight by the waves: planks of wood, barrels, crates, cans and bottles. The boy took all these things home.

One morning, however, he found no flotsam and jetsam. Something was not the same as usual. The boy looked all round the bay, but there was nothing to be seen. Then a dark shape did catch his eye, a shape far out in the shallow water. It must be a rock, the kind known as an erratic block, washed out of a sandbank by the sea during the night. So that was what was different. The boy felt relieved.

But then he thought, surely this rock would have been visible earlier – there'd have been surf breaking over it, and a rock this big doesn't just suddenly appear out of nowhere. I'll go and take a look at it. And he waded slowly out into the shallows.

The boy walked round the rock which had risen from the sand, marvelling. As yet there was no danger to fear from the tide, for the wind was blowing off the land and out to sea, but the boy still felt uneasy. He sensed a strange gaze behind him, as if he were being watched. He looked round, but no, he was alone. The seagulls soared high overhead in the wind. All was calm out at sea. The boy turned back to the rock again.

A deep sigh stopped him in his tracks, a sigh which seemed to come from the rock itself. The boy examined the rounded mass of stone more closely, and then he saw the eye. It was in the rock, just above the water, and it was looking at him. An ancient eye, wide-open, gazing at the boy in silence.

The boy looked back in astonishment. At last he tore himself away from that stare, cupped his hands to scoop up water, and poured it carefully over the open eye like salty tears, to keep it from drying up in the wind blowing off the land. He had no idea why he did that; he was simply thinking, where do you come from, and who brought you here?

Then a quiver ran through the rocky mass, and a soundless thought reached the boy's mind, *I was looking for you – you who are different from the others, my friend – and now I've found you.*

The boy stood silent and amazed.

Don't you remember – a hundred years ago, when I was as

small as you are?

The boy shook his head and moistened the open eye with water again.

I came into this bay. I wanted to play, but then something caught me and tugged at me. I reared up, I turned and struggled and pushed against it, but it was no use. Invisible seaweed was holding me prisoner, binding me more and more tightly. Something pulled me into the shallows, and I was drawn up and out of the safe darkness of the deep water. And then at last I saw them.

They walked upright. There was seaweed on their heads and they wore skins.

They dragged me over to a place among the rocks where the cliffs coming down to the sea form a basin which holds water even when the tide goes out, and fills up again when it comes back in. I resisted, but they were stronger than I was.

One of them picked up something sharp and jabbed it into my flesh. I couldn't escape. Others came and hit me with sticks. I sank down to the bottom of the basin, but their sharp spears still pricked me. Why? I wondered. Why are they doing this?

And then, in the night, you came. You and the others. I was afraid, but when you saw my wounds the sea ran out of your eyes. I came up to the surface and you stroked me. You and the others — they were as small as you still are. You sang to me softly, and you felt sorry for me. You cut the invisible seaweed and showed me the way out of the basin, so that when the bigger ones came back my prison was open. 'Swim away!' you whispered. 'Swim away! They're coming to kill you!'

I have looked for you ever since that day. You haven't changed at all, but I have grown old. I wanted to see you once again, to thank you and say goodbye.

Screaming, a gull dived low over the boy's head, and he started with surprise. The tide! He had to get back to the beach before the water rose any higher. The eye in the rock was already underwater; no danger threatened it now. I must have been dreaming, thought the boy. He ran over the sandbanks and back to the beach as fast as he could go.

'Did you see it?' asked his father when he came in through the doorway.

'See what?' asked the boy.

'They say there's a whale stranded down in Donegal Bay.'

'A whale?' said the boy.

'It's a hundred years ago that anyone last saw a whale in our bay,' said his father. 'My great-grandfather used to tell the story. A young whale it was, caught in the fishermen's net. They pulled it out of the sea and into the basin over by the cliffs. My great-grandfather was a boy at the time; he said the fishermen were going to slaughter the whale and boil its blubber down for oil to burn in their lamps. But the children felt sorry for the captive animal, perhaps because it was only a child still itself, and they helped the little whale to escape from the basin by night. My great-grandfather got a sound thrashing for his kindness at the time. It's a story he often told me.'

The boy stared at his father and finally asked, 'Is it a true story then?'

'Of course,' grunted his father. 'If you don't believe me, look in the church records, or ask old Conroy. His grandfather was among those children too. So did you find anything saleable down on the beach?'

'No, nothing,' the boy replied, and he said no more.

It was some time before Bambert came back out of this story to real life, to find himself still in his kitchen. Just possibly, he said to himself, just possibly that boy picked up his own story from the beach where the hot-air balloon had carried it.

Perhaps he found the remains of the balloon and asked his father what they could do with it.

And perhaps his father dried Bambert's letter off, read the story and then wrote back. Yes, that must have been what happened. Bambert felt so sure of it that he didn't need to read the letter which had come from Ireland with his story. He put the sheets of paper with the tale of *The Eye in the Sea* into an empty folder, hoping that his other ten stories would come back to him too.

Next morning Mr Bloom the shopkeeper was surprised to find that Bambert had eaten all three of his breakfast rolls and didn't send any of them down in the lift again. He thought this was a good sign.

Bambert had less than a week to wait for the second story to arrive. Mr Bloom brought it up to him in person. Bambert, who was happily eating breakfast in his dressing gown, quickly cleared the table to make room for his letter, and looked curiously at the stamps. They said España and had a picture of the king of Spain on them. The sender's name and address was: Maria Gonzales-Oliva, Calle del Palacio Moro, Cordoba.

As soon as Bambert took the story out of the envelope he forgot all about Mr Bloom the shopkeeper, who closed the door quietly behind him, leaving Bambert alone with his mysterious letter.

Bambert smoothed out the manuscript, wrote in 'Cordoba' where he had left a space for the scene of the story, and added the name 'Guadalquivir', because he remembered from his schooldays that both Cordoba and Seville lay on that river. So now the title of his story was *The Princess of Cordoba*:

THE PRINCESS OF CORDOBA

The ancient city of Cordoba lies on the River Guadalquivir in Spain. The Palacio Moro, the Moorish palace, belonged to an Arab caliph more than a thousand years ago, and stands there to this day.

The caliph had a daughter who was as wise as she was beautiful. According to custom and tradition it was time for her to marry, but the Princess of Cordoba had no intention of agreeing to take a husband chosen for her by anyone else. So she set her suitors a task: she said she would marry no one but the man who brought her the key to the truth as his gift.

On the day when the suitors arrived, all the streets of Cordoba were decorated. Magnificent barges were hauled up the River

Guadalquivir. Proud and noble horses pranced through the streets pulling golden coaches. Banners and pennants hung from all the windows, and crowds lined the road to the palace as the suitors made their way towards it in a festive procession. Inside the palace, everyone was whispering in excitement. The princess sat next to her father in a silver chair. She was holding a lorgnette – a pair of glasses mounted on a stick – and gazing intently through it at the golden double doors.

The heralds blew a fanfare, and the murmuring and the rustle of skirts in the room died away. The double doors were opened, and the lord chamberlain announced, 'His Excellency Count Valpolicella, from the golden city of Venice, wishes to present the princess with the key to the truth!'

The caliph nodded graciously, and the princess bent her wise little head to invite the guest in.

Count Valpolicella was extremely magnificent, and his pages were carrying a cask of the finest Valpolicella Superiore. 'Dulce Princesa,' began the count, making a very elegant bow, 'in vino veritas.'

The heralds translated, 'Sweet Princess, the truth is in wine!'

The princess smiled. She looked at the Venetian count, his cask and all his finery. Then she lowered her lorgnette and asked her noble suitor to drink the wine in the cask all by himself. It took him some time, but the princess was patient. When she raised her lorgnette again, she saw that the count was completely intoxicated. 'Dulshshsh . . . Prinshshsh . . .' he babbled, and then his pages

had to carry him out.

No sooner had what remained of Count Valpolicella's truth been mopped up from the floor than the lord chamberlain announced the arrival of the second suitor, 'His Excellency the Crown Prince to the Nabob of Kush!'

The crown prince had come from the Himalayas on an elephant. He had a heavy chest brought in and placed before the princess.

'Loveliest of lotus flowers!' he cried. 'I bring you the key to the truth!' Then he lifted the lid of the chest. The caliph's ministers and councillors stood there dazzled, for the chest was full to the brim with gold. Everyone stared spellbound at this rich gift. But the princess frowned and said, 'I can buy all kinds of things with gold, but as the key to the truth it is no use at all. Truth that must be bought has an unpleasant touch of falsehood about it.'

'So what?' said the Crown Prince of Kush.

'Exactly!' replied the princess.

The Crown Prince of Kush closed the chest again, and the ministers and councillors sighed regretfully. 'If you don't mind,' the princess told them, 'I'm the one who would be marrying him, not you! Very well – next, please!'

The Crown Prince of Kush left the palace feeling confused. What was the meaning of that little exchange? 'So what?' he had said, and, 'Exactly!' she replied. He climbed on his elephant, the chest was hauled up behind him, and the crown prince began his journey home. The people in the streets were silent. A rejected suitor is always a sorry sight, and easily provokes mockery, whereas the crown prince was used to being greeted with shouts of joy, so he opened his chest and flung handfuls of gold into the silent crowd.

'Hurrah! Hurrah! Hurrah!' cried the people in delight.

'So what!' laughed the crown prince. And from somewhere or other a softly whispered, 'Exactly!' reached his ears.

Meanwhile the heralds were blowing yet another fanfare. The lord chamberlain announced the arrival of the third suitor, 'His Excellency Polycrates, Heir of the Blood Royal to the Tyrant of Samos and Icaria!'

Polycrates entered. He put a covered wicker basket down in the middle of the throne-room, and looked around him with a watchful eye. Then, slowly, he raised the cloth which was laid over the basket. The ministers and councillors retreated, for a number of venomous snakes reared their heads, writhing above the brim. The Heir of the Blood Royal to the Tyrant put the cloth back over the basket. With a bold gesture, he pointed to the ministers and councillors and said, 'The key to the truth is fear!'

The princess sat as if spellbound, hidden behind her lorgnette. There was an awkward silence, and the Heir of the Blood Royal to the Tyrant of Samos and Icaria bowed.

'The truth,' he said calmly, 'the truth is as great as the pyramids of the Pharaohs. Those pyramids were built out of fear – the fear of death. All that is great and good proceeds from fear: light from the fear of darkness, language from the fear of silence, writing from the fear of oblivion. The power of rulers depends on the fear they inspire in others.'

The princess raised an interested eyebrow. This did not escape the Heir of the Blood Royal to the Tyrant of Samos and Icaria. 'And anyone on earth,' he added, 'will reveal truths which are still hidden for fear of the torturers.'

The ministers and councillors flinched, and half the court turned pale. They were all secretly thinking, if she marries this Polycrates it will be the end of me! The princess saw the terror felt by her obsequious courtiers, and said nothing. This short silence of hers, she thought, would rid the court of dishonesty, gossip and corruption, intrigues and secret machinations for a long time to come.

When the courtiers had suffered enough, and were already fearing the worst, the princess said aloud, 'That will do. Take your basket of snakes back to Samos and Icaria, please. My kingdom is not so great that we need to build pyramids. Nor do I like torturers. Their truth is the greatest betrayal of all. Fear, yes indeed, fear is a mighty force. Mightier still, however, is Amor, the smallest of the gods. Would any children be born otherwise? Every woman fears the pain of childbirth. Yet wives embrace their husbands and give their children little brothers and sisters. The smallest among the gods conquers the greatest fear. Go away! I do not want to feel your cold touch on my skin!'

The ministers and councillors breathed a sigh of relief. Polycrates turned pale and went out, his gaze fixed. The crowds in the streets cried, 'Hurrah! Hurrah!' expecting more money. But

Polycrates cleared the streets with his whip as he drove his coach along, and only the bravest fools and jesters in Cordoba dared to make faces behind his back.

'Next, please!' sighed the princess.

The lord chamberlain hesitated. The heralds looked embarrassed. The ministers and councillors exchanged glances. How could they tell the princess without hurting her feelings? There *was* no next. All the other suitors had made off, some discouraged by the wealth of the Crown Prince of Kush, others in fear of Polycrates. But most of them had fled before the wisdom of the Princess of Cordoba.

She herself appeared very composed, and hid behind her lorgnette, so that the laughter in her eyes would not give her away.

Bambert caught himself thinking that he would have liked to serve the princess as her court jester. But the days when dwarves were kept at courts as fools were long gone. A pity, thought Bambert, for he could have given a great deal of good advice.

Deep in his heart, Bambert had fallen in love with the Princess of Cordoba as soon as he made her up. He had not known then, however, that she lived in Spain, but it seemed quite right for her to be the daughter of a Moorish caliph who ruled the Arab part of that country. Not only did Europeans learn to calculate in Arabic figures from the Moorish masters of Spain, the Arabs also taught them the arts of medicine, architecture, mathematics and astronomy. The Moors were thought to have invented spectacles too; at that time lenses were ground from beryl crystals. A clever people and a wise princess. Bambert sighed. His head sank heavily to the table top, and he fell asleep.

He dreamed he was in the gondola of a hot-air balloon being carried by moderate north-easterly winds straight to Cordoba, where it came down gently in the palace courtyard. The Princess of Cordoba received him most graciously, and thanked him for delivering her in his story from the hard-drinking Count Valpolicella, the swaggering Crown Prince of Kush, and the chilly heart of Polycrates.

'It's the least I could do!' said Bambert modestly, turning red. But then a spirit of mischief came over him, and he asked whether the princess had yet found the key to the truth herself.

The princess laughed aloud, took Bambert in her arms and kissed him. No one had ever in his life embraced and kissed Bambert so tenderly before. But just as the princess was running her fingers through his hair, saying, 'Oh, but the key to the truth was your own idea!' the herald entered, knocking his staff loudly on the floor. 'Next, please!' he cried, and Bambert woke up.

However, the knocking continued until Bambert got up from the kitchen table to open the door. There stood Mr Bloom with an envelope in his hand. 'Guess what, here's the next letter already!' he said. Bambert was not fully awake yet, and hardly noticed that this time the envelope bore his address in Cyrillic lettering.

'Looks Russian to me,' said Mr Bloom, who had learnt Russian long ago as a child.

'Can you read it to me?' asked Bambert, who had woken up properly by now.

'I don't know if I can still remember how,' said Mr Bloom, 'but I'll have a go.'

'I think there's a Russian dictionary somewhere here,' Bambert recollected, and he went to his library to find it.

But by the time he came back into the kitchen Mr Bloom had already deciphered the sender's name and address: Alexander Korshunov, Cultural Secretary, Ministry of Education and Literature, the Kremlin, Moscow, Russia.

'Well done, Mr Bloom!' said Bambert, and at that moment he almost forgot the Princess of Cordoba. There was only the faintest touch of red in his face to betray the fact that just a few minutes ago a princess had been kissing him.

'You ought to drink more fluids, Bambert,' commented Mr Bloom. 'Plenty of fluid is good for hot flushes. I'll send you something up straight away!'

Bambert nodded absent-mindedly, and Mr Bloom went back down to open his shop. Bambert couldn't wait to find out which of his stories had chosen the Kremlin in Moscow as its setting. Opening the envelope, he found the tale of *The Moving Light* inside.

It was the work of a moment to emend the manuscript: 'kings' became 'tsars', 'the citadel' became 'the Kremlin', and the name of the city where the story was set was now 'Moscow', the place where it had come to rest after a long flight carried on the westerly winds.

Bambert waited a moment for the kitchen lift to come up with a crate of sparkling mineral water from Mr Bloom, along with a bottle of red wine which he had not expected.

He couldn't help smiling, and decided to keep the wine for later that evening. Then he poured himself a glass of sparkling water, and began to read:

THE MOVING LIGHT

Tsars once lived and ruled in the ancient city of Moscow, which is still the capital of Russia today. Some of the tsars were good and some were cruel. It was under the cruel tsars that Russian writers and poets suffered persecution.

For those who told the truth about such tsars were beheaded. And if they wrote nothing but fairy-tales instead, to avoid telling lies, they were thrown into a dungeon for failing to praise the tsars enough. Their dungeon lay beneath the paving stones of an inner courtyard in the Kremlin.

So there sat the Russian poets and philosophers in deep darkness, living on bread and water. Just once a day, when the sun above the Kremlin was at its height, a sunbeam fell into the vault for a few short minutes through a hole in the dungeon ceiling. It cast a patch of light on the straw covering the dungeon floor. The light moved over the straw, reached the opposite wall, climbed higher and then was gone.

Just once a day, and only if the sun was shining.

One day, the sunbeam cast its patch of light on the straw as usual. As it moved slowly towards the opposite wall, the prisoners thought they saw a child sitting in the island of light. A child writing something in an open diary.

At first all the prisoners thought the sight was a hallucination, a delusion, so no one mentioned it, until in the end one of them asked, 'Did the rest of you see that child too?'

Then all of a sudden they knew that what they had seen was real.

The prisoners grew restless, and shook the iron bars to summon the guards. 'Let that child go!' they cried. 'Let the child go if you have any heart at all!'

'Shut up!' bellowed the guards. 'Are you out of your minds?' And they shone their torches into the dungeon vault. 'There's no child here. The Tsar would never allow such a thing. If there's a child in there, let's see it for ourselves! Come forward, child, and then we'll let you go.'

But no child came forward.

'There you are, then,' said the guards, going away. They took their torches with them, plunging the prisoners back into profound obscurity. Every one of them had seen the child, but there was nothing visible now in the darkness of the dungeon.

Next day, when the sun cast its island of light on the straw again, the child stepped out of the darkness, sat down in the light, and opened the diary. Writing all the time, the child followed the sunlight as it moved across the floor, climbed the opposite wall, and then was gone.

'What were you writing?' one of the men asked quietly, in the darkness.

'I'm telling my diary the story of our escape,' the child replied.

'You mean you're planning to escape?' said the man, horrified. 'But they'll catch you, and you'll pay for it with your life.'

'We're all going to escape,' said the child firmly. 'I've written the story already.'

'Read it to us!'

'Tomorrow,' said the child. 'Tomorrow, when the light comes back.'

The prisoners had seldom waited so impatiently for the day's single ray of sunlight. At last the patch of light began moving over the straw, crept across the floor, and fell on the child's open diary. Then the child read the story:

'Once upon a time there was a dungeon deep beneath the Kremlin courtyard, a dungeon which even the prison guards did not like to enter. A single ray of sunlight kept faith with the prisoners, passing through the darkness once a day, and a child saw it.

'The child, who was keeping a diary, wrote, "We are all going to escape on this sunbeam. It will give us light and carry us all away. We shall be lifted out of this prison and taken to an island of light where the way to freedom lies open ahead of us. All the prisoners here, full of the spirit of liberty as they are, will escape the power of the dungeon on that sunbeam."'

And then the patch of light disappeared from the dungeon wall. The old prisoners, the poets and philosophers, were silent, deeply moved. Many of them were weeping quietly. They did not want to contradict the poetry of the child's tale. Why deprive a child of hope, even if such hope belongs only in fairy-tales where good always defeats evil?

But next day, when the ray of light began moving through the dungeon again, the child suddenly shouted in a piercing voice, 'Guards! Treachery! Mutiny!'

The guards immediately raced up and opened the cell door. 'Don't any of you move!' they shouted. Then they saw the light falling into the dungeon and wondered where it came from. And what was that on the straw in front of them? One of the guards picked up the child's diary and began to read it aloud. The others came up and crowded round the diary too. Did anyone ever read such stuff? 'We are all going to escape on this sunbeam.' And then, 'It will give us light and carry us all away.' What stupid nonsense! Escaping on a sunbeam? How totally ridiculous! The guards roared with laughter, slapping their thighs.

Then the dungeon door slammed shut behind them, it was bolted from the outside, the warders were trapped, and the prisoners made their escape.

It was two whole days before anyone in the Kremlin up above noticed that the dungeon guards were missing. A search party set out, and they were found shut up in the dungeon and set free. They were talking wildly: something about an imprisoned child and a sunbeam. And they produced a diary saying ridiculous things like, 'We shall be lifted out of this prison and taken to an island of light.'

The guards were sacked.

And up in the Kremlin courtyard, a loose paving stone which no one had noticed before was put back in its place.

Since that day, no ray of sunlight has ever moved across the floor of the dungeon below.

Bambert opened the kitchen door and took a deep breath, as if he had just succeeded in escaping from the dungeon himself.

He had written that. He had set the child and the poets and philosophers free – with a ray of sunlight! The knowledge that he was capable of doing great things, in spite of his deformed body, ran through him.

In this happy mood, Bambert found his corkscrew and opened the bottle of red wine Mr Bloom had sent up to do him good.

There was not enough wine in the bottle, of course, to make Bambert another Count Valpolicella, but he had to celebrate his victory over the prison guards in the Kremlin dungeon!

Not surprisingly, Bambert slept a deep and dreamless sleep that night. Perhaps he even snored. Next morning he slept right through the arrival of the fresh breakfast rolls and the post sent up by Mr Bloom. It was not until nearly midday that he woke, went into the bathroom, and found himself looking at the reflection of a Bambert with a slight hangover in the mirror above the washbasin.

'Cheers!' said Bambert to his reflection, raising his toothglass to it.

In his dressing gown, he made his way to the kitchen, took the rolls out of the lift – they had gone cold long ago – and looked at the post.

Two letters had arrived this time. Two letters on the same morning! Bambert rejoiced. And like a child saving the best morsel for last, he left the letters unopened and ate a hearty breakfast. Not until he had cleared away the coffee things and the marmalade, by now feeling strengthened and refreshed, did he return to the two letters.

One of them came from France, the other from Italy. Which should he open first? Which story should he begin with?

Bambert decided in favour of France, which may have been something to do with yesterday's bottle of wine – a 1992 Châteauneuf-du-Pape.

The envelope had been posted in Paris, and the sender's name and address ran: Jean Baptiste Cordonnier, Number 16, Quai d'Orsay.

Bambert conscientiously put these facts down in his story, which was the tale of *The Silken Scarf*.

THE SILKEN SCARF

Once upon a time a cobbler in Paris had an apprentice called Jean Baptiste. Jean Baptiste was a strange boy who could sit staring at the River Seine for hours on end. One day, however, he suddenly jumped up, raced back to the cobbler's workshop, dragged both the cobbler and his wife out of the house and into the street, and stood there trembling violently.

The cobbler and his wife were baffled by the boy's behaviour, and feared that he might have some serious illness. Just as they were wondering whether to take Jean Baptiste to see a doctor, never mind the cost, the house collapsed behind them with a roar like thunder.

The couple turned as pale as a sheet. Their apprentice had saved their lives! They embraced him silently, and determined that from now on he would be like their own child to them. The boy shed no tears at the sight of the ruined house, but just stared ahead of him until, with a deep sigh of relief, he returned to the present. He was glad to see that his master and mistress were still alive – and as for them, they guessed that Jean Baptiste had the rare gift of being able to see into the future.

One day Jean Baptiste was sitting on the banks of the Seine again, staring at the water, when a bottle came floating by. The boy found a stick, brought the bottle in to the bank, and fished it out of the water at the Quai d'Orsay.

The bottle was corked, and there was a silken scarf inside it. The boy uncorked the bottle and took out the scarf. When he spread it out, he saw that there was writing on it in fine brush-strokes. With growing amazement, Jean Baptiste read the words on the silken scarf: 'This scarf,' they said, 'will be fished out of the water by the cobbler's apprentice Jean Baptiste at the Quai d'Orsay, around noon on the fourteenth of July in the year 1851.'

Once again the curious feeling that had made the boy tremble came over him. He ran home and asked, 'Is it the fourteenth of July today?'

'Why do you ask?' inquired the cobbler. 'Of course it's the fourteenth of July, and so it will be all day long!'

'And is this the year 1851?'

'Yes, and that'll be the date all year!' laughed the cobbler.

Jean Baptiste examined the silken scarf, and found the label of a scarf-maker from the Quartier Versenne sewn into it. He hurried off to that part of the city and found the shop. Yes, the scarf-maker told him, he did indeed remember who had bought the silken scarf: a very clever gentleman, maybe a philosopher, who taught his pupils down in the cellar of Number 16 on the Quai d'Orsay. Three years ago, it had been. He remembered so precisely, he said, because he had enjoyed a long conversation with this gentleman on the question of whether it was possible for a human being to foresee the future.

Jean Baptiste thanked the scarf-maker and went down to the Quai d'Orsay, where he found Number 16 and saw a door standing open in the yard. He entered a vaulted cellar. When his eyes were used to the dim light, he saw a coffin standing on a bier in the middle of the vault, with mourners seated on benches round the walls. Wax candles flickered in the corners of the cellar. Then a young gentleman came up and spoke to him: 'You must be Jean Baptiste, the cobbler's apprentice. Our master has been expecting you, but sad to say you come too late, he died last night. He gave us this book for you.'

And the young gentleman handed the boy an old book. Jean Baptiste thanked him, stood beside the coffin for a little while, and then left the vault.

He sat down on the banks of the Seine and opened the book. Near the front, between the pages, he found a letter:

Dear Jean Baptiste,

We shall never meet in this world now. But I know that you are poor. Dig in the cellar of the house where you

live, and you will find a passage. It leads to the catacombs below the city, and behind the first walled-up niche a treasure is waiting for you. Make good use of it. And never forget: even the wisest of soothsayers cannot escape his own future.

Farewell, Jean Baptiste.

The boy closed the book and ran home. He climbed down into the cellar and knocked on the walls. Sure enough, they sounded hollow in one corner. He dug up the cellar floor at that spot, and found an iron trapdoor. When he pulled it up, he saw the entrance to an underground passage. Taking a torch, the boy set off along it, and was soon in the catacombs below the city. He made his way carefully forward, stopping when he came to the first walled-up niche. He could loosen the crumbling brickwork with his bare hands, and his fingers, feeling behind it, encountered a lead-bound casket. He took it out and climbed back to the cellar, where he opened the casket. It contained louis d'or and Spanish ducats, enough to last a lifetime! And there was a note on top of the gold coins.

It read:
Jean Baptiste

Share this treasure with the poor, since you will be executed for having it in your possession. Make haste!

There is not much time left. And remember: even the wisest of soothsayers cannot escape his own future.

The boy was terrified. Why should he be executed for giving gold away to the poor? Surely that was no crime? Yet so far all the philosopher's predictions had been right. The boy was afraid to climb out of the cellar with the treasure, but then he heard men's voices talking hoarsely down in the catacombs. 'It'll be this way! No, further on. Let's hope the casket's still there. Go on, it must be further along!'

The voices seemed to be coming closer. The men were looking for the treasure he held in his hands, and if they found him here in the cellar they would kill him. He couldn't stay where he was. Jean Baptiste closed the iron trapdoor, pushed a heavy barrel over it, and climbed the cellar steps.

On that day, the fourteenth of July in the year 1851, the beggars under the bridges of Paris feasted to their hearts' content; they had more than enough to eat, they drank the finest wine, and they told the strange tale of a cobbler's apprentice who had been handing out gold coins to them, until in the end the police had arrested him and thrown him into prison. The boy claimed that he had not stolen the gold but had found it, and he stuck to his story. However, the police did not believe him.

Only the beggars guessed that the boy had not lied to them. But who believes the word of a beggar?

When Bambert put his story of *The Silken Scarf* aside he wondered why he hadn't saved the boy's life. Surely he could easily have let Jean Baptiste the cobbler's apprentice escape his pursuers instead of being thrown into prison?

On the other hand, it was only through the letter from Paris that Bambert had discovered where the story was set and when, for it happened almost a hundred and fifty years ago.

When Bambert looked at the envelope from Paris again he gave a start of surprise, rose, went to his study and came back with a magnifying glass. He examined the stamps on the envelope through this magnifying glass for a long time. There was no doubt of it: they were postmarked 1851!

Bambert already suspected that his stories had sought out not only the place, but also the time of their setting. But could it really have been Jean Baptiste himself who had sent this letter off to him, Bambert, from back in the year 1851?

The sender's name provided food for thought as well: as he had seen, it was Jean Baptiste Cordonnier, and *cordonnier* is the French word for a cobbler.

He would have to discuss it with Mr Bloom. Mr Bloom knew all about stamps; he collected them in albums, and was proud of his almost complete collection of European postage stamps.

Bambert picked up the letter from Italy. The stamps were right again, but these were new, and postmarked in Venice. He would keep them for Mr Bloom. Looking at the name of the sender, Bambert saw that a woman, Donna Silvia Crespo, had found this story. The lady's handwriting was as elegant as her address: the Palazzo Bertini on the Canale Grande.

Bambert took his manuscript out of the envelope and wrote in 'Venice' as the scene of the story, adding the names of the 'Palazzo Bertini' and 'Silvia Crespo'. It was his tale called *Frozen in Time*.

FROZEN IN TIME

The most famous looking-glass ever made in Venice hangs in the Palazzo Bertini, where the tall round-arched windows look out on the Canale Grande, the gondolas, and the vaporettos carrying freight.

The picture of a very beautiful girl is frozen in this mirror.

Beneath the portrait in the looking-glass, which appears to be covered by a fine network of lines, stands a heavy old table, and every evening an old gentleman with hair as white as snow and an extremely ugly young woman sit there and dine together in silence, by the light of a branched candlestick.

The old man with snow-white hair is Crespo, the famous merchant, and the ugly young woman is his granddaughter Silvia. But who, you may ask, is the beauty frozen in the mirror, looking down on this strange scene from behind the fine veining of lines?

The story began when the merchant Crespo's granddaughter came to live in the Palazzo Bertini. Only the two of them and a devoted servant occupied the place. The girl had lost her parents, and the old merchant was the last living relation she had.

As his granddaughter grew up and her beauty began to unfold, the old gentleman told his servant to hang black cloths over all the mirrors in the dining-hall. For in her grandfather's eyes, the young girl's beauty represented sin and temptation.

That was how the girl came to grow up in the Palazzo without ever seeing her own reflection. She knew herself only from inside her mind, and had no idea how beautiful she was.

One night, however, an autumn storm raged over the Venetian lagoon, doing a great deal of damage in the city. It tore a shutter in the Palazzo Bertini off its hinges, and the shutter broke a window. Once the storm had made its way into the Palazzo, it howled through the rooms, rattling the double doors and blowing the black cloths away from the tall mirrors.

Next morning, when the merchant Crespo's granddaughter came to sweep up the broken windowpanes in the mirror-lined hall, the black cloths had been swirled up into a heap in one corner of the room. But the girl paid no attention to them; she had to pick up the shards of glass and be careful of small splinters.

Then, suddenly, she saw another girl opposite her, bending down to pick up broken glass as well. The girl stopped in amazement. Why did no one ever tell me, she wondered, why did no one ever say there was another girl living in this house?

Believing she had stumbled upon a well-kept secret, the girl pretended not to have noticed the strange child, and merely cast her surreptitious glances. The girl opposite her seemed to be doing the same.

So they both swept up the shards, and they both carried the

broken glass out of the mirror-lined hall, going in different directions. When she had reached the double doorway the girl turned. She waved to the child opposite, and the child opposite waved back.

Feeling pleased, the girl carried her broken glass down to old Crespo's servant in the kitchen. The other girl will arrive with her own broken glass in a minute, she thought, and she waited expectantly. But no other child appeared.

'What are you waiting for?' asked the servant.

The girl felt as if she had been caught in some guilty act. 'Oh, I was only wondering whether you wanted me to bring down the black cloths too – the wind tore them off the walls.'

'The black cloths? Torn off the walls?' The servant was alarmed. 'Did you see what was behind those cloths?'

The girl thought of the other child, and did not want to give her away. Perhaps she was hiding there in secret. 'What would there be to see?' she asked out loud. 'I was busy picking up the shards and splinters of broken glass from the windows. The floor was covered with it! I wouldn't have had time to look at the walls of the hall!'

The servant believed her, muttered an excuse, and left the kitchen. He hurried up to the mirror-lined hall, found a ladder and hung the black cloths over the mirrors again. They gave the hall a rather mournful look, robbing it of its festive appearance and spacious proportions.

But now the girl knew there was a secret double door hidden behind one of those cloths, and the other girl, the one who had

waved to her, lived behind it. Who was she? What mystery surrounded the child who had been picking up broken glass like herself, but couldn't come into the kitchen? Why had her grandfather kept the child hidden from her for so long?

The girl's longing for the secret friend who could not show herself grew stronger and stronger.

Old Crespo did not fail to notice the change in his granddaughter. 'Has she looked behind any of the cloths?' he asked his servant. 'I seem to see her standing at the double doors leading to the mirror-lined hall rather often. Lock them, and keep the key on you all the time! In no circumstances do I want her looking into mirrors before she's grown up!'

The servant promised to obey.

He locked the mirror-lined hall and kept the key on him. He wondered what was going on, however, when the girl asked if there was another child in the Palazzo, a girl the same age as herself. As she spoke, the girl looked hard at the servant, and his tiny movement of momentary alarm did not escape her.

One day at noon, when the servant was having a siesta in his room, the girl stole the key to the forbidden hall from his jacket, which he had left hanging over a chair in the kitchen. She ran barefoot upstairs, unlocked the double doors, and found herself standing in the mirror-lined hall. All the mirrors were covered up, except for the one facing the double doors. Its black cloth had slipped off again, perhaps because the wind had blown it away, for the broken window had not yet been replaced.

And there in the double doorway opposite stood the other girl. She hesitated. She waved. Then both girls ran towards each other, arms outstretched, shouting with delight at the joy of their reunion.

There was a terrible crash, followed by a shower of splintered glass as the girl ran into the mirror, out of which the other child was running towards her. The broken glass cut her beautiful face. The sound woke the servant and his old master, and they hurried upstairs, only to find the girl bleeding in the middle of the splintered glass.

'Why did you do it?' cried the girl in distress. 'Why did you hide that girl from me? Why wasn't I allowed to see how lovely she is? Where has she gone? What have you done with her?'

There was no reply; old Crespo was struck silent by rage and fury. And his granddaughter was disfigured for life by the cuts from the splintered glass.

But when the broken mirror was put back together, the picture of the girl's beauty as it once was seemed to have been frozen into the glass. Behind the network of cracks and crevices, it looked even more mysterious than in life.

The girl forgave her grandfather. But she insisted that every evening they must sit at the dining-table in silence in front of that innocent beauty, until the picture disappeared from the looking-glass.

That day would never come, however, until the proud, obstinate merchant Crespo uttered a truly sincere apology for failing to see anything in his granddaughter's youth and beauty but sin and temptation.

There was so much pain in this story that it made Bambert think of his own tormented childhood. He still suffered from the after-effects of all his countless operations. Bambert hoped that some day before the end of his life the bitter old merchant Crespo could overcome his coldness of heart, the coldness which still kept that fraction of a second of time frozen in the shards of the looking-glass.

Bambert knew what it was like for only your inner self to be beautiful because you were deformed on the outside.

Yet it had been he who let the girl run into the mirror in his story. He, Bambert, had not stopped her. Perhaps because he loved that girl too, but was bitterly aware that such a beautiful girl would never love him in return?

Deep in such thoughts, Bambert began to suspect that it was not old Crespo who ought to apologise to his granddaughter, but he himself, Bambert, who had pulled the strings of the story . . .

If so, then he would have to go to Venice and explain everything right from the start. He would have to apologise with all his heart, until the moment frozen in time disappeared from the mirror above the dining-table in the Palazzo Bertini.

While Bambert was suffering from a guilty conscience, Mr Bloom was sitting over his stamp collection, looking for unpostmarked English stamps with the portrait of Queen Victoria, great-great-grandmother of the present queen of England.

When he had found the stamps he took them out of his album with a pair of tweezers, moistened them with a sponge, hoping their glue would still work, and stuck them on the envelope he had ready.

After that Mr Bloom did his accounts, which as usual showed that his grocer's shop was not really profitable any more, although that did not bother him, since he had in fact retired some time ago, but he hadn't wanted to give up the shop entirely. What else could he do that would keep him mixing with other people? As a landlord, luckily, Bambert didn't charge the usual rents for the Old Town because he liked to have Mr Bloom living near him, or that would have been the end of Mr Bloom's grocery store, both retail and wholesale.

Over the years Mr Bloom and Bambert had become friends. Theirs was a friendship with its own little rituals, one in which neither tried to get too close to the other. Live and let live, that was the tacit agreement between them.

Mr Bloom had known Bambert's parents, and when they asked him to keep an eye on their son after they were no longer around, he promised without hesitation. He liked the odd little fellow who lived above him and made up stories, and it made him sad to think how much pain Bambert sometimes suffered, while there was nothing he could do to help. Such a little body, thought Mr Bloom admiringly, but such a great spirit.

Now he put Bambert's post in the lift, waited a moment, then took it out again, switched off the light in the shop, locked up, and went round to the back.

Next morning Bambert found a letter from England in the lift. From London! Bambert thanked the east wind for blowing his own letter that way, found that he couldn't read the sender's name, and opened the envelope. He recognised his tale of *The Waxworks Cabinet*. Bambert entered 'London' as the setting, and made the river which flows through that city the Thames; he turned 'the Queen' into 'Queen Victoria', 'the murderer' into 'Jack the Ripper', and 'the poet' into 'Lord Byron'. They all fitted into his story beautifully!

THE WAXWORKS CABINET

An old, old house stands in London on the banks of the slow-flowing River Thames, the walls of which once accommodated the world-famous Waxworks Cabinet. A cabinet of this kind means a display of wax models of famous people. The waxworks look so real you might think they were alive, for they are exactly the same in size and appearance as their living models.

One day, a boy came down to the banks of the Thames, sat on the quayside wall and dangled his legs. He had nothing to eat and no money. When he looked down at the water it was as if he were wondering whether it might be a good idea to throw himself into the river.

But he liked life, and he couldn't help being poor.

Then a stocky, stout little gentleman approached the boy. He had been watching him, and now he raised his top hat and spoke. The boy looked awkward, but finally he stood up and followed the stout little gentleman. They walked along the banks of the Thames until they reached the old, old house and went inside. The stout little gentleman's office was next to the front door; he left his top hat there, and then went downstairs with the boy to the vault containing his Waxworks Cabinet.

At the sight of the first wax figure the boy politely raised his cap. The stout little gentleman laughed. 'No need to ask how they are! Try touching them – they're stone-cold, nothing but wax dummies.'

'What will my work be here?' asked the boy.

'I've lost my manservant,' said the stout little gentleman. 'He was my butler, and he looked after the waxworks too. They have to be kept clean, you see, dressed and groomed just like real people. The smallest grain of dust would destroy the illusion. You'll even have to wash them now and then. That's your work, and I'll pay well for it!'

The stout little gentleman led the boy upstairs again, back to his office. He was breathing heavily. He opened his desk drawer and gave the boy an advance.

'All that money?' The boy stared in amazement.

'Yes, yes, that's all right,' said the stout little gentleman. 'Go and get something to eat and drink, and buy yourself some new clothes. When you come back I'll show you where you're to sleep.'

The boy solemnly promised that he would indeed come back, and then went into the city. He had a good meal in a tavern, for he really was very hungry, and he bought himself new clothes. After that he hurried back to the old, old house by the Thames, where the stout little gentleman was waiting for him. He showed the boy a recess on the staircase with a bed in it, and then sent him off to begin work.

The boy went downstairs to the waxworks. He dusted their faces with a feather duster. He wiped them clean with a damp cloth. He polished their shoes, adjusted their wigs, powdered them and sprayed them with perfume. He worked hard and did his job well. When he came to the poet Lord Byron and was combing his lordship's hair, a gold coin fell to the ground beside him. The boy jumped. He looked round. There wasn't a soul in sight, but the gold coin was genuine. Had one of the visitors to the Cabinet lost it here? But it seemed to have dropped just that moment. The boy felt uneasy.

He came to the waxwork model of Queen Victoria. The boy carefully wiped the queen's face and applied fresh rouge to her cheeks. He coloured in her lips with red lipstick. He straightened her wig and smoothed out the folds of her full skirt. When he bent to tie the queen's shoelaces he thought he felt a hand gently patting his head. It was a perfectly distinct feeling! The boy straightened up. No, there was nobody else here, only the waxworks. Had a draught of air deceived him? But could a draught of air get down here to the cellar? Had he perhaps touched the sleeve of the royal dress with his head?

The boy decided to take better care.

He turned to the next waxwork, the figure of the once notorious murderer Jack the Ripper, standing next to the queen. The boy washed the wax figure's right hand, which was clutching a murder weapon, the knife he had used to kill his victims.

When the boy had cleaned the hand and the knife, he freshened up the blood on the blade with red paint to make it look as real as possible. Visitors to the Waxworks Cabinet liked a good fright! Then, all of a sudden, the boy cut himself on the blade of the murderer's knife. It was a real blade, and sharp. He flinched, feeling as if he had seen a curious gleam in the eyes of the waxwork.

With a shudder running down his spine, the boy collected his cleaning equipment and went upstairs to see the stout little gentleman. He had to find out for sure what was going on!

The door to the stout little gentleman's office stood open, and the boy went in. The gentleman was sitting at his desk, but when the boy spoke to him there was no reply. The boy came closer. He touched the stout little gentleman's hand, and then let go of it in horror, for it was as cold as clay. He had touched the hand of a waxwork. What on earth was all this?

The boy ran to the front door, but it was barred. He tried to force it open, but the strong lock held firm. So the boy turned and went slowly downstairs again. He heard merry music coming up the stairs towards him! Quietly, the boy approached the entrance to the vault.

When he finally went in he found the whole pale, waxen company having a party. Queen Victoria was the first to recognise him. 'There you are at last, my page!' she cried. She gave him a hug and thanked him for looking after her so well earlier in the day.

Lord Byron composed a short poem and dedicated it to the boy – in gratitude, said the poet, for his kind attentions.

Even Jack the Ripper thanked him, especially for putting a new drop of blood on the blade of his knife. He had to admit, he said, that he had a passion for blood. Not just any blood, oh no, it must be human blood. Jack the Ripper laughed loud and uproariously, and then was contrite: 'Sorry, me lad, sorry, never meant to scare you.'

The boy felt paralysed by horror. A servant was offering food and wine with a knowing smile. It seemed that the boy had been invited to the party and must join in. He felt as if he were in a dream. He danced and drank and danced and drank, until he staggered and fell to the floor exhausted. As pale as ashes, he lay there with all the colour drained from his face.

Next morning the waxworks were standing stiffly in their places again, and a new one had joined them: a beggar boy sleeping by the quayside.

But a stout little gentleman was visiting the shop where the beggar boy had bought his new clothes, asking, 'Can you take these clothes back, please? My errand boy bought them from you yesterday, but I'm afraid they are all too tight.'

Then he went down to the banks of the Thames, where a young woman was sitting staring sadly at the water. The stout little gentleman went up to her and courteously raised his top hat . . .

Very British, thought Bambert, who was extremely fond of English crime and horror stories, and shared the English liking for black humour. He wouldn't mind visiting London himself some day, complete with butler and Rolls Royce. Bambert enjoyed the touch of malice in the story too. He had been brought up to be a good boy and show gratitude the whole time. 'Or you'll always lose out!' his parents kept telling him. Bambert must be well behaved. Bambert must give in to other people. Bambert mustn't argue. Bambert must never lose his temper.

But what did you do with your anger, then? What did you do with your

desire for revenge, for bittersweet chocolate, for forbidden fruit?

At least in his stories Bambert could let himself go, alarming even himself.

And afterwards he felt better.

'I can't help getting angry, though!' he had often told his parents. But he soon realised that when he lost his temper he looked like Rumpelstiltskin, so what his parents said was right: he'd always lose out.

Bambert sent a note down asking if Mr Bloom would be kind enough to come upstairs for a few moments. When Mr Bloom closed the shop for lunch and came up, Bambert showed him the stamps from Paris with the 1851 postmark, and asked if they could possibly be genuine.

Mr Bloom looked at the stamps long and hard. Then he said, 'As far as I can see those stamps are indeed genuine. Very interesting stamps. Rare, too. Where did you get them?'

Bambert only sighed and said, 'Well, now I have a riddle to solve.' He did not answer Mr Bloom's question, for he wanted to keep his secret to himself, and the time did not seem ripe for revealing everything to his old friend. But since he knew that Mr Bloom was an enthusiastic stamp collector, he offered him the six envelopes which had arrived so far. 'Here, you have them,' he said. 'You can keep the stamps or swap them, whichever you like.'

Mr Bloom thanked him. 'But haven't I seen these stamps somewhere before?' he asked.

Bambert nodded. 'Of course! You put my post in the lift for me.'

'Yes, so I do!' Mr Bloom struck his forehead with his hand. 'But that would mean that ever since 1851 a letter . . . ' He didn't finish his sentence. Bambert nodded, baffled: it was indeed incredible. There was no understanding it . . . Mr Bloom decided to say no more, and quietly went away. He was only thankful that he had taken the old English stamps with the picture of Queen Victoria off yesterday's envelope again. In any case, the adhesive no longer stuck. The sight of those rare old English stamps could only too easily have aroused Bambert's suspicions.

Luckily he already had modern British stamps in new pence values in his album. They stuck well and gave away no secrets.

Mr Bloom opened his shop again, said good afternoon to Mrs Feldman, who had been a faithful customer for years despite the attractions of supermarkets and discount stores, and set about re-stacking the shelves with canned fish, which had sold surprisingly well over the last few days. Mrs Feldman counted out her money at the till, then dug about in her shopping bag, searched for something, located it, and handed Mr Bloom an envelope. She had found it near the old summerhouse up in her orchard, she said. Mr Bloom thanked her, and added the envelope to the others he was keeping in the drawer underneath the till.

That evening, just before shutting the shop, Mr Bloom took two envelopes from the drawer round to the back where he lived. Late that evening he could be seen sitting over his stamp albums again, magnifying glass in one hand, tweezers in the other.

Bambert spent a very restless night. He had hardly slept at all. For breakfast, he brewed extra-strong coffee, so strong that it was drinkable only with plenty of milk. He had a long, cold shower to wake himself up. A little later, he opened the lift in the kitchen and took out three breakfast rolls and two letters. One of the letters was from Bosnia; the second was another letter from France, postmarked Bayonne. A north-easterly wind must have guided this story on its way. Unhesitatingly, Bambert opened the letter from Bosnia first. It had been

posted in Sarajevo, obviously carried there on a north-westerly wind. When Bambert had taken his story out of the envelope, smoothed the paper flat and saw which of his tales had made its way to Sarajevo, he felt a lump in his throat. It was the tale of *The Strange Game*:

THE STRANGE GAME

Not long ago, the city of Sarajevo was under siege in a terrible war. Marksmen on the heights around the city fired at it from above. Its inhabitants crept into their cellars for shelter, and all the roads around Sarajevo were closed. No bread, no meat, no flour, no milk – no food at all was allowed into the besieged city. The people inside were starving.

During the day, they emerged briefly from their cellars to breathe fresh air. It was dangerous, for the snipers up on the mountains shot at anything that moved in the city below. They fired rifles, howitzers and shells.

One morning, a child came out of the door of one of the cellars, which were barricaded with sandbags. He crouched down in the dust, playing with a little stick, and seemed to be drawing something on the ground.

Not two minutes had passed before a second child came out to call the first one in again. 'What are you doing out here so long? Playing target practice or what?'

'I'm drawing a picture,' said the child crouching on the ground.

Then an explosion shattered the morning air, and once again a nearby building went up in flames. The child with the stick said, 'Boom!' and drew the ruined house in the dust with a few strokes.

'Are you mad?' cried the child standing beside him. 'You're to come in at once, before those men up in the mountains train their sights on you.'

The child in the dust did not answer.

Yet again there was a flash in the mountains above the city, and a shell hit an empty high-rise building down below. Smoke rose into the sky, and the thunder of the explosion shook the city in the valley.

'They've hit the high-rise building,' said the child playing with his stick in the dust. He drew the outline of the building and then made a gaping hole in it with his stick. The high-rise building in the dust broke up.

'Come back down into the cellar!' shouted the child standing beside him.

'I can't!' the child crouching on the ground shouted back. 'I have to finish this game. Now I'm playing that the next shell hits that factory!'

And he drew the factory on the ground and stuck his stick into it, swirling up the dust.

'Bang!' he said. 'Crash!'

Sure enough, at that moment, a shell did hit the factory, and black smoke rolled towards the sky.

'You see?' said the child crouching on the ground. 'I haven't finished yet, but it won't take long!'

'Come in!'

'I tell you, I haven't finished. I must play the game to the end!'

'Oh, stop it, do stop it and come back in!' begged the child standing beside him.

'Not now,' murmured the child who was playing his game, 'not now. You can see it's no good. I'm much too near the end.'

The standing child was in despair. 'What makes this game you're playing in the dust so important that you won't come in?'

'I'm playing war,' said the crouching child, 'but I'll soon have finished.'

'Finished what, for goodness' sake? Finished what?'

Then the crouching child raised his head and said, 'Leave me alone! I'll be through with it in a moment.' There were tears in his eyes.

'Why are you crying?' asked the standing child.

'Because you won't let me finish the game! I'd almost done it!'

'But I'm not stopping you! I've just been told to fetch you back into the cellar, that's all. Do you want to be shot dead?'

Then the child crouching on the ground threw his little stick away in a rage and returned to the shelter of the cellar. The child who had been sent to fetch him in followed, his shoulders drooping. Inside, their grandmother put her arms round both children. She asked no questions, but waited.

'I so nearly did it!' sobbed the child who had been playing.

And his grandmother asked, 'Did what?'

The child stammered, 'To start with, I was only playing at what had already happened. I played with the stick in the dust and drew what had happened on the ground. Then I thought of something that might happen. And it did. I drew it on the ground and then it happened.

'I didn't notice what was going on at first, but when I'd drawn the factory in the dust it was hit too. Just the way I'd drawn it. Then I suddenly knew that from now on everything I drew in the dust with the stick would come true. Just the way I drew it!

'So I was going to draw the end of the war. With the men in the mountains going home so that we could come out again and play properly, the way we used to. And the sun shining and the birds singing, and everything just like it was before. I wanted to draw that, oh, I did want to. And it would have happened! I so nearly did it . . .'

The old woman hugged her grandson to her breast. She shed no tears, she spoke no words. She held the boy in her arms for a long time, and then, looking up, she saw her other grandson grieving and said at last, 'You can't help it. That's the way he is. You did nothing wrong. Perhaps he'll be a great artist some day if we survive this war. He believes in the power of his pictures. You can't help it. And he can't help it either.'

When the picture of the two Sarajevo children in Bambert's head had finally faded he still felt a lump in his throat which would not go away.

How many wonderful pictures had wars devoured before they could be painted? How much music had they swallowed up before it could ever be heard? How many of the arts had they crushed before they could fulfil their promise? How many great ideas still slumbering in small children had wars destroyed?

War is the father of all things, a famous scholar once said. But little Bambert did not agree: since when have fathers eaten their own children?

Bambert felt unable to open the second envelope just yet. He went up to the attic window and stared out. The day was gloomy and overcast, with heavy rain-clouds in the sky. Bambert stayed by the attic window weeping.

When he had shed all his tears it was evening, and Bambert crept under the bedclothes. He curled up like a child and fell into a deep, consoling sleep.

The envelope from Bayonne lay unopened on the kitchen table.

Next day after breakfast, when Bambert picked up the envelope from France and tore it open, he smiled. He smiled because this was a more comforting story than yesterday's. It was his tale of *The Flight of the Dolls*. And because the story had found its home in France, Bambert now called it:

THE FLIGHT OF THE DOLLS FROM PARIS

The Côte d'Argent is a long strip of coastline in the south-west of France. Its fine sand and high dunes stretch from Arcachon in the north to Bayonne in the south. The surf is strong here, for tall waves roll in from the Atlantic Ocean to break on the beach.

A little girl from Paris went there with her parents one weekend.

They wanted to enjoy the fresh sea air and take a holiday from life in the big city. It was spring, and a brisk wind blew drifts of sand low over the beach, piled up dunes, and sent the spray of the surf falling like drizzling rain behind them. The child trudged through the fine sand with her parents, all three of them making only slow progress. The little girl in her red anorak kept stopping and bending down to pick up seashells, empty snail shells and smooth stones.

Meanwhile her parents walked ahead, talking to each other. They were so deep in conversation that they lost sight of their child. When they finally turned round to look for the little girl, she had disappeared. Her mother and father were terrified. They called to their daughter, but she did not answer. The parents turned round on the spot and ran back, until at last they saw the red anorak among the dunes. They were immensely relieved. Their child was sitting in the sand, playing, oblivious of all around her.

'What made you sit down here all of a sudden?' asked her mother. Without looking up the little girl replied, 'I must make them better again.'

Her parents looked at each other, and her father gently tried to disillusion her: 'No, dear, the seashells are empty and the snails aren't living in their houses any more. That's the way it is. No one can make them better again!'

But the little girl looked up and said, 'Something bad happened.'

'Did you hurt yourself?' asked her mother.

'It didn't happen to me,' said the little girl impatiently. 'It happened to my babies. Look!'

And the little girl picked up a doll's arm, a single arm. 'It came off. I have to make them better.'

Her father was about to say, 'Oh, all right, just this one, and then come on!' But the words died away in his throat. For there were parts of dolls scattered all over the beach: here a little pink arm stuck out of the sand, there several tiny legs lay entangled with each other. There were heads and bodies too. It was as if the sea had cast up a family of a hundred dolls on the sand. The little girl gathered up separate piles of arms and legs, heads and bodies, and put the naked little dolls back together again one by one.

'Whatever happened to you all?' she asked as she worked, comforting her babies. 'Never mind, Mummy will make you better again.'

When each doll was complete she put it down on the sand in front of her. The circle of small, naked dolls grew larger. Soon the child had mended over ten of them. Her baffled parents stood and watched. There was something disturbing about this dolls' graveyard in the sand, although all it contained was parts of dolls: pink plastic parts. Their daughter sat among them, patiently fitting the parts together. Now there were over fifteen little dolls, all pink and naked, sitting round the child in the sand. There would soon be a great many more if she went on like this.

'Whatever happened to you, babies?' the little girl kept asking. But the dolls did not reply. They only smiled.

'Perhaps there was a shipwreck?' said the child's father, trying to make sense of it.

'If there'd been a shipwreck, they'd be wearing life-jackets!' said the little girl.

'Perhaps they were swept out to sea by the breakers when they were bathing?'

'But if they were bathing they'd be wearing swimsuits!'

'Well, suppose a storm washed a beach stall selling toys into the sea somewhere?'

'But they don't sell dolls naked in separate parts from beach stalls!'

Whatever explanation her father tried, the little girl rejected it. As she came to the twenty-fourth doll, she looked up and said, 'There's a war going on somewhere.'

'Nonsense,' said her father. 'Who would make war on dolls?'

'So who tore off their arms and legs and heads?' asked the little girl indignantly. Her parents said nothing. The child went on putting the dolls back together.

Finally she asked, as if in surprise, 'Why don't you two help me?'

'All right, I'll help you,' said her father, and he went to pick up the parts of the dismembered dolls.

Her mother sensed what was coming. 'You don't intend to take all these dolls home, do you?' she asked cautiously. For by now almost thirty little dolls sat there smiling in the sand.

'They've got to live somewhere.'

'Not with us!' said her mother. 'I mean, your room is full of grown-up dolls and baby dolls already . . .'

'These dolls can't possibly go back!' said the little girl indignantly. 'Just see what they did to my babies there!' And she held up a pink, bare, dented doll's leg.

'There isn't room for them at home,' her mother was about to say. But when she saw how upset her child was she kept silent, feeling somehow guilty.

'There you are, that's all I could find,' said the little girl's father, putting the rest of the dismembered dolls down on the sand in front of his daughter. She fitted them all back together again.

That evening, forty-three little naked pink dolls were driven back to Paris from Bayonne lying on the back seat of the car. The little girl was asleep in her child seat with a happy smile on her face and one last doll on her lap, a doll with one arm and one leg missing.

Bambert felt proud of that little girl! He had always wanted children, but he had never met a woman, a real flesh-and-blood woman, who would have liked to marry him. So Bambert's sons and daughters all lived in his stories.

Bambert was particularly fond of the little girl from Paris, because she made people better. Sometimes Bambert made up names for the children in his stories. This little girl was called Odile, but only Bambert knew it.

Perhaps he might tell Mr Bloom about his children some time. Mr Bloom was a good listener.

And Mr Bloom never laughed at Bambert's odd ideas, which followed his physical urges and were behind all his brief escapes into dreams and stories.

One day, Bambert knew, the time would come for him to tell Mr Bloom all about himself. Then it struck him that he hadn't yet thanked Mr Bloom for the bottle of wine which gave him such a good night's sleep.

Meanwhile, Mr Bloom himself was sitting down in the shop to read the story Mrs Feldman had brought from the orchard where one of Bambert's hot-air balloons had become stranded after its brief flight. After reading it, he realised that Bambert was possessed by a great desire to undo the worst things he knew about. Small and deformed as he was, Bambert wanted to save the world from its own horrors. Mr Bloom guessed that Bambert felt he had to save himself too, for the story he had just been reading was set at a time when deformed people of small stature were murdered in concentration camps, killed by doctors who failed to keep their oath to act only for the good of their patients.

After much thought, Mr Bloom decided to put a set of Polish stamps and a Polish postmark on this story. He remembered the city of Slubice, lying opposite the German city of Frankfurt an der Oder, just the length of a bridge away across the river. Yes, that would do.

Next morning, Bambert found two envelopes in the lift which had come up to the kitchen, one from Poland and the other from the Hohentwiel area in Swabia.

The Polish postmark said 'Slubice', and looking at the atlas, which was now his constant breakfast companion, Bambert saw that the city of Slubice lay on the River Oder on the border between Germany and Poland, opposite the city of Frankfurt an der Oder. Bambert entered the name of the river, and realised that some benevolent spirit watching over his stories had brought this one to its proper place too. Bambert was pleased, because it was the tale of a successful escape. It was called *The Glass Rafts*, and where he had left the setting of the story undecided, he now wrote in the names of the 'River Oder' and the city of 'Slubice':

THE GLASS RAFTS

Just outside the city of Slubice, there are hollows and depressions in the ground which stir unhappy memories in older people. Only the River Oder, quietly flowing by, knows just what happened beyond its embankments in the days of the Black Angels of Death. At least, they felt to themselves like angels. They were dressed entirely in black with a death's-head badge, they marched in shiny black boots, and they cast a mortal chill around them wherever they went.

One day back in this time, the River Oder heard a strange procession approaching. The sound was like the tread of children's feet, stumbling along rather than walking. They made fast progress, but they were weak, and they were not going anywhere of their own free will, but running from something behind them. The hard tramp of shiny black boots at the back of the line of children drove them on. The Black Angels of Death were herding the children ahead of them. The procession stopped when it came to the banks of the Oder, and only then did the river see the flock which the Black Angels of Death had driven through the night. Yes, they were indeed children, going barefoot although it was winter and bitterly cold. Children with strangely old faces and shaven heads, thin children in convicts' clothing, wearing jackets and trousers like flimsy pyjamas. There was fear in the children's eyes.

'Go on! No stopping!'

The orders barked out by the Black Angels of Death sounded as

harsh as the tread of their boots. They were armed, and they alone knew where they were all going. They were herding their flock to its journey's end, where an open pit lay ahead of them: a pit which would be visible later only as a slight hollow in the ground. The children were driven along the banks of the Oder with blows from cudgels. Those who fell were helped up by any who could still walk, for if they lay where they had fallen, they were lost.

The Black Angels of Death knew no mercy. They had their orders and they obeyed them. For angels, even black angels, are always obedient. There was no doubt at all that they would drive their flock on to the very end. Multiplied a hundredfold, the shadow of fear hastened ahead of them, settling frostily on the roads and making the hearts of the Black Angels beat in time with its chill. It was not far to the pit when a shouted 'Halt!' reached the children's ears. The flock obeyed, freezing. The children shifted from foot to foot, crossed their arms over their chests and shivered. Where had all the warmth of life gone?

The Black Angels stood aside. Cigarettes glowed. Metal clinked on metal. The Black Angels were stopping to draw breath. One last great effort lay ahead of them, and after all, they had children of their own. They drank brandy from hip flasks. As the brandy went down their throats, it burned away any pity which might have made their task more difficult. The little flock on the banks stood shivering in the cold.

Then the waters of the Oder began to flow more slowly, as if the river were holding its breath. The cold shadow cast by the Black

Angels did not spare the water, but slowed it down, delaying its current and making the surface smooth. And solid ice now formed on those sluggish waters, ice floes that drifted to the bank one by one. The ice floes knocked against each other, scraping on the stones of the river embankment. They drifted downstream like glass rafts on the slowly flowing river, and the mist grew thicker.

There stood the Black Angels of Death, smoking and taking a breather before driving their flock the last part of the way to the open pit. There was little time left.

Cigarette ends were already being ground out by shiny black boots. The ice on the River Oder grew thicker. The floes crowded closer together. Ice floe by ice floe – raft by raft.

The ice was thick enough to bear the weight of a thin child, but too fragile to take an adult.

Thick enough for the weight of a thin child?

Too fragile for an adult?

The shivering flock began to grow restless. The first child was already running out on the ice. Blindly, the second child followed. Then, suddenly, they were all jumping on to the ice floes in the river. Desperation and fear drove the very last of the children to take refuge on those swaying rafts.

Curses were heard from the bank, but the mists swirled together, so thick that you couldn't see your hand before your face, and when the Black Angels of Death fired shots they missed their mark.

The river was flowing faster now. The Black Angels of Death tried to venture out onto the ice, but in vain. Their shiny black boots broke

through it. The ice carried the children away, but would not take the soldiers.

Now the children were drifting downstream towards the mudflats and the marshes – the impenetrable marshes.

But Little Father Frost had laid frozen roads and bridges over the marshy land. The children made their way to the isolated cottages of the fenland farmers and fishermen, who gave them food and kept them hidden. The people living in these humble dwellings helped the children to get away: away from the Black Angels of Death. For a thaw set in next morning, and no pursuer could pass over the frozen roads and bridges which had been there the night before.

Bambert knew only too well why he had left it to the river and Little Father Frost to save the children in his story. In those days, most people couldn't be expected to give children from the camps any help. They didn't want to know. They preferred to look the other way. Only a few were brave enough to resist, and many of those few good people paid for their courage with their lives.

Bambert sighed, for he knew that he himself would probably not have survived then. He thought of the deformed little teacher from Holland, Alexander Katun, whose skin can still be seen as a lampshade in a concentration-camp museum full of such horrors. Bambert shivered. He had gooseflesh.

He had a very good idea why he preferred to imagine himself back in a more distant past: he would rather be a jester or fool, acting as a mocking mirror held up to an aristocratic court, than be born at a time and into a society so possessed by a deluded belief in its infallibility that it would tolerate no fools.

Bambert knew by heart the names of famous dwarfs who had been court fools and jesters: Perkeo, court jester and dwarf in Heidelberg Castle; Stanislaus, court dwarf of Cardinal Granvella in Brussels; Morgante, court dwarf of the house of Medici in Florence; Robin, court dwarf of the Countess of Arundel; Sir Jeffrey Hudson, court dwarf to Queen Henrietta Maria of England; Sebastian de Morra, court dwarf and fool to King Philip IV of Spain.

And did not even the French Academy of Sciences owe its existence to a court jester, the dwarf at the court of Julie d'Angennes who later became Bishop of Grasse, His Eminence Anton Godeau?

The little Bishop of Grasse in Provence, in the South of France, had been a great writer as well as a clever man, and Bambert secretly modelled himself on Godeau the dwarf, who once said, 'Writing is an author's paradise; the first revision is purgatory.' And was not Bambert himself now making the first revision of his own stories?

Perhaps Bambert let all these things pass through his mind only to get himself into the mood for his tenth story, the last but one: there were still two stories to come, and Bambert knew that one of them must be his tale of a fool. As for the eleventh and last story, which was still unwritten, he hoped it would tell itself.

So which of those two stories was waiting in the still sealed envelope? The address it came from was in the Hohentwiel region of Swabia, which told him that it must be the tale in praise of the fool, unless that story had failed to find its way to the place where it was set.

Bambert opened the envelope, and was not disappointed: he found his story entitled Red Stockings, Black Coat.

RED STOCKINGS, BLACK COAT

The mountain of Hohentwiel rises at Singen in Swabia. Once upon a time, a count lived there who raided the farmers' cowsheds to steal their cattle, and plundered their barns and cellars. The farmers were left destitute, without food or even seed corn. Then the land was stricken by a terrible drought. People and animals alike starved. Cows collapsed and died in the meadows, pigs perished in their sties. Even the rabbits were thin, and only the carrion crows grew fat. They flew over the parched fields in black flocks, a noisy company of mourners, feasting on dead bodies.

One of the farmers' boys noticed them. Like all the other children, he had hardly grown at all that year because he was suffering such hunger. The boy noticed that all living things around him were dying of famine, except for the crows and the Count of Hohentwiel, who did not seem to be affected, and he wondered why.

There was nothing to be done about the count, but the boy thought: well, if I'm to survive this famine I must learn from the crows, or I shall die too. So he put on a black jacket and long red stockings, climbed a tree and perched there among the crows. He watched them and learned their language.

At sunrise, he heard the crows sending out scouts, 'Any deaths anywhere? Go and see if something died overnight!'

The scouts flew off, and came back later to say what they had seen: a dead cow in the meadow, a starved pig in its pen, a horse fallen in a field beyond the village. Then the crows rose into the sky in a great crowd, and wherever they came down they gorged themselves on the dead.

The boy had learned what he needed to know. He climbed down from the tree and put a cow's skin over his head. Then he lay down behind a cowshed. Along came the fat crows, ready to peck his eyes out. 'Got you!' cried the boy, and he seized the fattest birds and roasted them on the spit, leaving the other crows in a state of great consternation.

Next morning, the boy covered himself with a horse's skin and lay down in the ditch beside the road. Along flew the crows, ready to peck out his eyes. 'Got you!' cried the boy, and he seized the fattest birds. He roasted them on the spit and ate them up. Well, they were better than nothing. Now the crows were afraid. 'We shall never get the better of this fellow,' they said to each other. 'Let's hear what he wants from us.'

The boy, who understood their language, climbed up to join them in the tree.

'Why are you eating us?' asked the crows.

'Because I'm hungry,' said the boy.

'Why don't you get your own kind to give you something to eat?'

'Because my own kind are all starving, and there's no food to be had,' replied the boy.

'That's not true,' said the crows. 'The cellars and stables of that merciless man the Count of Hohentwiel are full, and he has plenty of corn in the barns. He's one of your own kind – he's a human being!'

'But he's a count too!' pointed out the boy.

The crows consulted each other, and then they made the boy an offer. 'We'll hand the count over to you if you spare us in the future.'

'Very well,' said the boy, 'but if you don't keep your promise, I shall roast every one of you on spits cut from the last branches you perched on.'

The crows cawed, 'Never fear. A promise is a promise!'

So the boy spared the crows, stayed perching up in the tree, and waited.

Sure enough, the count came riding along. He galloped over to the tree, looked up and called, 'Hey, you there! You, the fool in the red stockings. What are you doing up there in that tree? Who are you? Speak up!'

'I'm the King of the Crows,' the boy called down. 'I was expecting you. I command you to open up the barns and give the starving people corn!'

The count laughed scornfully. 'A fool up in a tree, claiming to be King of the Crows? A fool who dares to give his count orders?' And he raised his crossbow to take aim at the boy. Then, out of a clear sky, a flock of crows attacked the count. He could barely defend himself as the crows kept pecking him. 'Call your crows off!' he cried, 'and we'll discuss it further!'

The crows withdrew.

But the count spurred his horse and rode away with a scornful laugh, so that his horse's nostrils foamed.

The boy signalled to the crows. They outstripped the horse, and there were so many of them that it shied and threw its rider. The count

crashed to the ground and lay there without moving until the boy arrived and stood over him. He tied the merciless count's hands behind his back, and led him back to his castle on the mountain of Hohentwiel at the end of a rope. The crows circled overhead.

On the way, the boy summoned all the people and made the count announce that the barns were going to be opened up. What he had taken from the people would be given back to them. The cowsheds and pigsties were flung open too, to provide the hungry people with meat, and beer and wine from the count's cellars were distributed. The barns were emptied as the peasants' grain and seed corn were given back.

Now a great crowd of people went up to the castle. Many of them were afraid, since it seemed unlikely that a fool would have power over their count for very long. Yet hunger was stronger than fear, just as a shirt lies closer to the body than a coat. The count saw the crows circling in the sky above him, and did as the boy said.

Only when the count had divided out and returned all the provisions he had stolen from the peasants did the boy untie him. The count rubbed his numb hands, and felt another fit of rage come over him. But the boy just pointed up to the circling crows in silence.

'Very well,' said the count, 'but even a fool like you must know that no one can bind his count with impunity! You call yourself King of the Crows, and you have taught me a lesson, which indeed is the duty and the value of fools. But a count is still a count! So I banish you to a mountain. It shall be your kingdom forever, and only there will your life be safe from me. And since you are ruler of the crows, they will be banished with you, and your mountain shall be known for ever as Crow Mountain.'

The boy agreed, and ever afterwards the mountain home of the peasant boy who had posed as a fool up in a tree, forcing his count to do his bidding, was known by that name. He was to be seen there for many years in his red stockings and black coat.

Some even believe he lives on the mountain to this day, but one thing is certain: the crows have remained true to their kingdom.

Bambert was glad of the little peasant boy's victory, and he remembered the name by which the little fool is still honoured today: Poppele of Crow Mountain.

So in the past fools were granted asylum, and a dwarf could become a bishop. Did Bambert have a single reason not to wish himself back in those times?

Bambert took his story and put it in the handsome folder on which he had written: *Bambert's Book of Missing Stories*.

Ten stories had returned to him now. Ten stories had sought out their settings and the characters who brought them to life. All he needed now was the last story, which was still unwritten and would surely write itself.

Bambert knew of eleven famous fools, and there were to be eleven stories collected in his book. He was planning to have eleven copies of it bound and sent to the people who had returned his stories from near and far.

The time had come to let Mr Bloom into his secret and tell him how much he was looking forward to the last story, which was still to arrive.

Bambert sent Mr Bloom down an invitation to visit him that evening. Mr Bloom replied in a note saying he was sorry, but he couldn't come today. He had a bad headache from too much thinking, but he would like to come another time.

However, Mr Bloom never seemed to get any better, and over the following days and weeks Bambert found himself going up to the attic window more and more often. He looked out over the city rooftops, and would not admit to himself that he was waiting for his last story, just as if it might suddenly float in through the attic window, still attached to its balloon, and bring his suspense to an end.

But the envelope he longed to see did not come up in the kitchen lift, the only post he had was bills, and his story did not fly back to him over the rooftops either.

None the less, Bambert put his faith in the kindly spirit which had accompanied his stories out into the world and back again, and he did not give up hope.

At the same time, he was anxious about Mr Bloom, whom he hadn't seen at all recently. It was as if he were avoiding Bambert.

Bambert decided to make his laborious way downstairs to Mr Bloom's shop to find out how he was.

When Bambert entered the shop through the back door, he found Mr Bloom in conversation with Mrs Feldman, whom he had known since he was a child. They both fell silent as he came in, and Bambert guessed that they had probably been talking about him.

Bambert gave them a friendly greeting and pretended he just wanted to buy a bottle of wine, a 1992 Châteauneuf-du-Pape if possible. Mr Bloom got up at once and went to the shelf where three bottles of this excellent vintage still stood. 'I can always put it in the lift, you know,' he said. 'You didn't have to come downstairs specially!'

'Oh yes, I did,' said Bambert. 'I'm still hoping you'll soon accept my invitation. So I need a good cognac too, and a box of cigars. I know you like to smoke a cigar.'

Mr Bloom felt embarrassed, and made haste to provide what Bambert wanted. Bloom's not looking too good, thought Bambert, and he asked, 'No post today?'

Mr Bloom shook his head regretfully, and Bambert climbed upstairs again. By the time he got there the lift had arrived in his kitchen with the wine and cognac, along with a little wooden cigar box which had an inviting smell.

Bambert had always hated waiting, and now he passed his time during the day studying the atlas, trying to remember which way the wind had been blowing when he let the last story float out of the attic window, the story which was to make itself happen.

Secretly, Bambert was living only for that final, unwritten story. The owls who soared soundlessly by night over the city rooftops found little clouds of smoke rising from Bambert's attic window. He had begun to smoke, and the cigars which were really meant for Mr Bloom dispersed in clouds of blue vapour above the city roofs. When Bambert ordered a second bottle of cognac from Mr Bloom, the shopkeeper knew that he was unhappy, and was obviously drowning his sorrows in drink.

Bambert developed dark rings under his eyes and lost his appetite again. Mr Bloom, who could tell his state of mind from the orders that came down, guessed that Bambert was waiting for one last story, but there was nothing he

could do to help until someone handed it in to him. So they were both waiting for the return of the last envelope, each in his own way. They both suffered from the slow passage of time, which suddenly seemed to be in no hurry at all, and they fretted with their own impatience.

Bambert was sure he had addressed the eleventh envelope in just the same way as the others: care of Mr Bloom, Retail and Wholesale Groceries. And Mr Bloom was sure that Bambert would not survive the strain he was putting on his own small health for long without doing it harm.

But neither the postman nor Mrs Feldman brought the waiting to an end. Mr Bloom sat looking at his stamp collection by night, prepared to provide stamps for any country in Europe. Bambert sat up at the top of the house under the attic window, staring out into the night with reddened eyes. Sometimes the cognac made him close his eyes, and he nodded off. However, the fresh night air always roused him again. Then Bambert felt alarmed and looked to see if his cigar was still burning, which would have been dangerous in the attic of such an old house. He was careful with the cigars after that, for the idea of suffocating up here in a smouldering fire horrified him. He wanted to be alive to see the return of the story which was to tell itself.

One night, the moon shone unusually brightly, and Bambert sat at the open attic window to drink in the sounds and shadows of the night, absorbing them like a sponge.

He admired the agility of the bats in flight, and their abrupt changes of direction as they sometimes fluttered just above him, close enough to touch.

He marvelled at the owls, never heard, and seen only when their shadows passed overhead. He was staring at the moon as it cast its pale and milky light over the rooftops when he saw something pale just below the attic window, not two metres away.

Bambert strained to see it better, and realised that something was caught on the eaves. The night wind moved it from time to time, but could not blow it away.

Suddenly the cognac fumes cleared, for Bambert realised that the thing caught down there was the envelope he was hoping for so much. The shadowy shape in front of it on the tiles must be the tissue paper which had once been a hot-air balloon, now soggy with rain. And didn't he hear the metal rim of the tea-light striking the gutter with a faint tinkling sound?

Bambert leaned far out of the window. He was trying so hard to make sure of what he was seeing that his eyes burned. His last story, the one he had sent out into the world on blank sheets of paper, the story he was waiting for so expectantly, was caught on the eaves in front of him – who knew how long it had been there, defying wind and weather?

Bambert reached for his stick, pushed a stool under the attic window and climbed into the window opening. No, the stick wouldn't reach the eaves. Bambert had to lean further out, one foot on the roof, his stick in one hand, his other hand clinging to the frame of the attic window.

Bambert needed to reach only a few more centimetres for the crook of his stick to catch the thread holding the envelope to the tissue paper, and he had almost done it when his foot began to slide over the tiles, the sharp edge of the window frame cut into his hand, and he let go in sudden pain. Then Bambert fell. Instinctively, he snatched at the envelope as if he could save himself by clinging to it, and then he lost consciousness.

Mr Bloom looked up from his stamp collection in alarm when he heard a slithering, bumping sound up on the roof, followed by a hollow thud. Running out of doors, he found Bambert lying motionless in the street, a sodden envelope in his hand. Bambert was still alive, and Mr Bloom shouted for help until a light came on behind the nearest windows and the neighbours called an ambulance.

Then everything happened very fast. Bambert was taken to hospital, with the ambulance siren blaring and blue lights flashing. Mr Bloom was in a state of shock, and not until he was back at home did he realise that he was holding Bambert's envelope.

Mr Bloom was so shaken and upset that he did not even notice the policemen standing in his kitchen. They asked whether he had a key to Bambert's flat, because they had to get in and see if there was anything to explain why Bambert had so unfortunately fallen out of the window.

Not until one of the policemen tapped Mr Bloom on the shoulder did he come out of his daze to some extent, and then he took the two officers up to Bambert's flat. They found an open atlas of the world and a half-empty cup of coffee on the kitchen table. They went on up to the attic window, where they found a full ashtray with the ends of several cigars stubbed out in it, and beside it, on a stool, an almost empty bottle of cognac.

The cigar ash was cold. The attic window stood wide open. There was no sign of any struggle.

The two policemen asked Mr Bloom to leave everything just as it was, so that their colleagues from the criminal investigation department could inspect the place tomorrow by daylight.

When the policemen had left the house Mr Bloom went up to Bambert's kitchen once more, and on the table, covered by the atlas, he found a stout cardboard folder with the words *Bambert's Book of Missing Stories* written on it.

Mr Bloom took the folder downstairs with him, cleared his stamp albums off the table, opened the folder, and found all the stories that his customers had been bringing into the shop over the last year.

He also found the opened envelopes on which he had written the names and addresses of the senders himself, in different handwriting each time because all Bambert's stories had come down in or quite close to the city, so it had been up to Mr Bloom to make Bambert's hopes and expectations come true. He saw his stamps again, the stamps he had used to confirm the credibility of Bambert's poetic faith in the power of his own stories. He saw the postmarks he had added to those stamps, lifting their impressions off real envelopes with a hardboiled egg before adding them to Bambert's letters.

And he held in his hand the unopened envelope, which still had no stamps and bore no sender's name and address.

Mr Bloom opened the envelope, and inside he found Bambert's letter, which he already knew by heart, and four blank sheets of paper.

All Bambert's desperate hopes had rested on these four blank sheets! Mr Bloom began to have a faint inkling of the great experiment on which his friend the little writer had embarked.

Tomorrow – no, today – Mr Bloom would tell the CID men it was possible that there might be traces of tissue paper and a tea-light on the roof, which would explain Bambert's fall.

It was gradually getting light outside when Mr Bloom went into the bathroom, shaved and showered, then dressed and hung a notice inside the shop door saying: Closed For The Day. Then he went to the hospital.

Bambert was under an oxygen tent in the intensive care ward. All kinds of apparatus was pulsating around him, tubes led into him, the respirator gurgled loudly, and Bambert's heartbeat and brainwaves flickered across two monitors. Bambert was hovering between life and death. Mr Bloom was not allowed to go in.

He told the ward sister who he was, and said he was still keeping a promise he had made to Bambert's parents. Would they please ring him if there was any change? The ward sister took down Mr Bloom's name and telephone number.

Mr Bloom went sadly home. And not knowing what else to do during this difficult waiting time, he opened the folder containing *Bambert's Book of Missing Stories* and read them, as a way of being close to his friend.

He read all the stories. And he read Bambert's thoughts about them, which he had noted down on the stories themselves. He had never felt so near to Bambert before.

Then the telephone call came, telling him that Bambert had lost his struggle with death.

Mr Bloom sat there feeling numb. He sat like that for two hours. Then he rose to his feet and lit a candle for Bambert. He stood at the table, poured himself a glass of red wine as if in a trance, raised his glass in farewell to his friend, and wished his soul an easy passage, that great soul which had now left a small and deformed body tormented by pain. Then Mr Bloom took the four blank sheets of the last story out of Bambert's folder. He picked up a fountain pen, for this was a story which had to be written with a real pen and ink.

Mr Bloom had never written a story before, nor did he feel he was a writer now. Perhaps he saw himself as someone doing his friend a last, loving service by letting a story use him to tell itself. *He* was simply writing it down. The candle in front of him burned with a steady flame as Mr Bloom began to write:

ON THE FAR SIDE OF THE DREAM

Bambert lay with his eyes open. He could scarcely move. He did not know where he was, but he saw tubes running into his arm. Above him hung a bottle from which time dripped into the tubes. Glowing points of light pulsated in the dimness. Bambert felt wires attached to his narrow chest. He tried to sit up, and fell back again at once.

A man's voice spoke beside him. 'You must drink. You must keep your lips moist.' Bambert felt a glass held to his mouth. He drank in small sips. Then he closed his eyes, and saw the attic window again. He climbed out of it and clung to the frame with one hand, while he pushed his stick down the slope of the roof with the other. He seemed to be searching for something; he seemed to want to pull some pale object towards him. Bambert felt himself slipping, he felt the sharp pain in his hand, but all the same he managed to grab the envelope.

After that he saw the faces of strangers above him. 'Lie still! Don't move. The ambulance is coming!'

'It's the thirst that's bad to start with,' said the voice beside him in the greenish twilight. The twilight smelled of seaweed and the salty waters of the ocean.

'Sleep now,' said the voice beside him. 'Sleep, don't move, keep still.' Bambert suddenly felt like a small child again.

'I can't move,' he muttered. 'Where am I? Where did those flickering lights come from?'

A curtain was pulled back. 'Get up, little man,' whispered a woman's voice. 'The time has come – you can't stay here! The ship has put in to shore. It's lying at anchor near the rocks.'

'What ship?' muttered Bambert. 'Who are you?'

'Please wake up, little man. We must make haste!'

Bambert got up and let himself be dressed. 'I was dreaming,' he said, 'and now I feel terribly thirsty.'

The lady's maid raised a glass of water to his lips.

'Slowly, drink slowly, or you'll choke!'

'Thank you,' said Bambert, but the lady's maid kept urging him, 'Sir, your ship is waiting!'

The ward sister came over to Bambert's bed. The male nurse beside it said, 'He's taking water, but his mind seems to be somewhere else entirely.'

The ward sister whispered, 'Please ring for me at once if there's any change in him.'

Then Bambert recognised the lady's maid – she was lady's maid to the Princess of Cordoba. 'Why are you tying me down?' he cried in alarm. 'Are we betrayed? What about the guards? Whose side are you on?'

The lady's maid smiled. 'Have no fear, all will be well. It's just to keep you safe, little sir.'

'I've taped his hands to the edges of the bed,' whispered the ward sister. 'He mustn't pull the tubes out.'

'But why?' asked Bambert in surprise, and the lady's maid replied, 'If one of the guards should see us, little sir, then he'll think you are a prisoner. This is just to keep you safe!'

'Have faith,' said the voice next to him, 'and all will be well.'

'If I am safer tied down,' Bambert heard himself say, 'then I'll put up with it.'

The lady's maid nodded. 'Come along, little sir. The time has come.'

His way of escape led into a long corridor, where drops of water trickled from the roof. The corridor seemed to be full of spider's webs trying to hold Bambert back. They clung around his breast, and the glassy notes of the waterdrops broke on the stone walls. 'Go on!' whispered the lady's maid, 'go on, don't turn back, little sir.'

Bambert groaned. 'Why do the bonds suddenly cut into my wrists so sharply?'

'Don't stop!' whispered the lady's maid. 'I'll take them all off later, little sir!'

At last, Bambert saw light at the end of the corridor. He pulled himself together. It couldn't be far now. He would soon be there!

The male nurse beside the bed saw the small, broken body arch upwards, and called the ward sister at once.

'Oxygen!' she ordered. 'Quick, he needs oxygen!'

And suddenly Bambert felt fresh air. The end of the corridor was quite close. That breath of fresh air was reassuring, and now at last he was in the light. Bambert narrowed his eyes to protect them from the sudden radiance. Ahead of him, he could make out a mighty shadow on the sea. The ship.

He heard a boat rowing up.

'Goodbye, little sir!' The lady's maid pressed a kiss on his forehead.

Bambert was rowed out to the ship in silence. When the rhythm of the oars died away, Bambert came alongside. Then the alarm was raised on land.

'Too late!' Bambert heard the lady's maid call. I'm safe, he thought. I got away again! He was standing on the ship with his eyes closed, he heard the rigging creak in the wind, he felt the ship begin to move slowly, its bows making out into the open sea. The sound of the alarm bells on land died away.

At last Bambert's bonds were removed.

'Welcome on board!'

Bambert opened his eyes, and suddenly he knew where he was: on the barge of the Bishop of Grasse, the favourite of Julie d'Angennes.

'I could not deny myself the pleasure of coming to meet you in person,' said the little man, and he took Bambert's hand to lead him into the cabin. They were all there on the barge, the whole company who had been waiting for him to arrive: his children Odile and Jean Baptiste, and his sweetheart the Princess of Cordoba.

'Why did you keep us waiting so long?'

'It's a long story,' said Bambert. 'I was on the far side of the dream. And while I was there – you in particular will like to hear this, my dear Monsieur Godeau – while I was there I wrote a book. A book of missing stories. I remembered you all in my stories.'

'Have you brought us the book?' asked Odile and Jean Baptiste in chorus.

'No,' said Bambert, regretfully. 'You can't bring anything across from the far side of the dream. They even tried to keep me there myself!'

'But now, thank God, you are back with us!' said the Princess of Cordoba, taking Bambert in her arms. 'Promise us never to go back to the far side of the dream again!'

Bambert looked over his sweetheart's shoulder at Bishop Anton Godeau, who shook his head circumspectly. 'No, it is not in our power,' said Bambert, and he fell silent and thoughtful. He sensed that the images of the far side of the dream were fading in him. But he knew very well that this side, the other side, was really here!

Mr Bloom laid down his pen, read through what he had written, and placed th last story in the folder with all the others. Luckily, thought Mr Bloom, luckily w still have his book. And he put out the light.